TULSA CITY-COUNTY LIBRARY

P9-AOZ-047

OCT - - 2022

EARLY BIRD
STORIES

Whoosh!

Early★Reader

First American edition published in 2023 by Lerner Publishing Group, Inc.

An original concept by Katie Dale
Copyright © 2023 Katie Dale

Illustrated by Letizia Rizzo

First published by Maverick Arts Publishing Limited

Maverick
arts publishing

Licensed Edition
Whoosh!

For the avoidance of doubt, pursuant to Chapter 4 of the Copyright, Designs and Patents Act of 1988, the proprietor asserts the moral right of the Author to be identified as the author of the Work; and asserts the moral right of the Author to be identified as the illustrator of the Work.

All US rights reserved. No part of this book may be reproduced, stored in a retrieval system, or transmitted in any form or by any means—electronic, mechanical, photocopying, recording, or otherwise—without the prior written permission of Lerner Publishing Group, Inc., except for the inclusion of brief quotations in an acknowledged review.

Lerner Publications Company
An imprint of Lerner Publishing Group, Inc.
241 First Avenue North
Minneapolis, MN 55401 USA

For reading levels and more information, look up this title at www.lernerbooks.com.

Main body text set in Mikado a. Typeface provided by HVD Fonts.

Library of Congress Cataloging-in-Publication Data

Names: Dale, Katie, author. | Rizzo, Letizia, illustrator.
Title: Whoosh! / Katie Dale ; illustrated by Letizia Rizzo.
Description: First American edition. | Minneapolis : Lerner Publications, 2023. | Series: Early bird readers. Green (Early bird stories) | "First published by Maverick Arts Publishing Limited"— Page facing title page. | Audience: Ages 5–9. | Audience: Grades K–1. | Summary: "Only one thing can ruin Ben's day outside: the wind. But Ben's dad has a plan!"— Provided by publisher.
Identifiers: LCCN 2021055146 (print) | LCCN 2021055147 (ebook) | ISBN 9781728438498 (lib. bdg.) | ISBN 9781728448374 (pbk.) | ISBN 9781728444628 (eb pdf)
Subjects: LCSH: Readers (Primary) | LCGFT: Readers (Publications)
Classification: LCC PE1119.2 .D359 2023 (print) | LCC PE1119.2 (ebook) | DDC 428.6/2— dc23/eng/20211130

LC record available at https://lccn.loc.gov/2021055146
LC ebook record available at https://lccn.loc.gov/2021055147

Manufactured in the United States of America
1-49672-49592-12/2/2021

EARLY BIRD
STORIES

Whoosh!

Katie Dale

illustrated by
Letizia Rizzo

Lerner Publications ◆ Minneapolis

Ben looked out of the window.

Dad's car was coming
down the road. Hooray!

"We're going to have a GREAT day, Dad!" Ben cried. "Let's go to the park!"

But just as they got to the park . . .

WHOOSH!

The wind blew Dad's hat off!

"Oh no!" cried Ben. He ran after it,
but it flew away.

"Never mind," said Dad.

"Let's have a picnic!"

But just as they got out
a bag of chips . . .

WHOOSH!

The wind blew the chip bag away!

"Oh no!" cried Ben. He ran after the chips, but they blew away.

"Never mind," said Dad.

"Let's feed the ducks."

But just as they got to the pond . . .

WHOOSH!

The wind blew the seeds away!

"Oh no!" cried Ben.

"Never mind," said Dad.

"Let's play ball."

But just as Ben kicked the ball . . .

WHOOSH!

The wind blew the ball into
a tall tree! It was stuck!

"Oh no!" cried Ben.

"Never mind," said Dad.

"Let's go home."

Ben was sad.

He went up to his room.

"What's the matter?" Dad asked.

"We could not have a picnic or feed
the ducks or play ball," Ben said sadly.
"The wind has ruined our day!"

Dad gave Ben a hug.

"The day is not over yet,"

said Dad, smiling.

"And a windy day is GREAT for . . .

. . . flying a kite!"

Ben and Dad went to a big hill.

WHOOSH!

The wind blew leaves all around them. It was fun!

Ben and Dad ran up the hill.

WHOOSH!

The wind blew Ben's coat like a cape.

"I feel like a superhero!" Ben cried.

When they got to the top of the hill, Dad held the string and Ben ran as fast as he could.

Then suddenly . . .

WHOOSH!

The kite flew high, high up into the sky!

"We did it!" Ben cried.

Ben smiled.

"This IS a great day after all!" he said.

Dad hugged him tight.

"Yes it is," said Dad.

Quiz

1. Whose car was coming down the road in the beginning?
    a) Ben's
    b) Dad's
    c) Mom's

2. What piece of clothing blows away in the wind?
    a) A scarf
    b) A hat
    c) A sock

3. Why can't Ben and Dad feed the ducks?
    a) They have the wrong food
    b) There are no ducks
    c) The wind blew the seeds away

4. What does Dad get out of his car?
   a) A new scarf
   b) A kite
   c) A ball

5. "This IS a day after all!"
   said Ben.
   a) Great
   b) Bad
   c) Fun

COLOR		GRL
Silver		L-P
Gold		K-L
Purple		J-K
Orange		H-J
Green		G-I
Blue		E-G
Yellow		C-E
Red		C-D
Pink		A-C

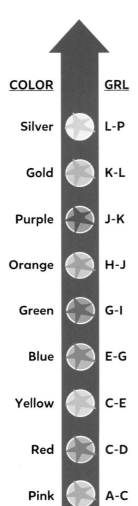

Leveled for Guided Reading

Early Bird Stories have been edited and leveled by leading educational consultants to correspond with guided reading levels. The levels are assigned by taking into account the content, language style, layout, and phonics used in each book. Visit www.lernerbooks.com for more Early Bird Readers titles!